W9-AVL-936

DOLPHIN OR PORPOISE?

By Rob Ryndak

Gareth Stevens
PUBLISHING

Please visit our website, www.garethstevens.com. For a free color catalog of all our high-quality books, call toll free 1-800-542-2595 or fax 1-877-542-2596.

Library of Congress Cataloging-in-Publication Data

Ryndak, Rob, author.
 Dolphin or porpoise? / Rob Ryndak.
      pages cm. — (Animal look-alikes)
 Includes bibliographical references and index.
 ISBN 978-1-4824-2712-7 (pbk.)
 ISBN 978-1-4824-2713-4 (6 pack)
 ISBN 978-1-4824-2714-1 (library binding)
 1. Dolphins—Juvenile literature. 2. Porpoises—Juvenile literature. I. Title.
 QL737.C432R93 2016
 599.53—dc23
                                   2014050048

Published in 2016 by
Gareth Stevens Publishing
111 East 14th Street, Suite 349
New York, NY 10003

Copyright © 2016 Gareth Stevens Publishing

Designer: Sarah Liddell
Editor: Ryan Nagelhout

Photo credits: Cover, p. 1 (background) Pakhnyushchy/Shutterstock.com; cover, pp. 1 (dolphin), 7 (dolphin), 19 (dolphin), 21 Ricardo Canino/Shutterstock.com; cover, p. 1 (porpoise) Jan Zoetekouw/ Shutterstock.com; pp. 5, 13 (dolphin) Willyam Bradberry/Shutterstock.com; p. 7 (porpoise) © iStockphoto.com/BrendanHunter; p. 7 (whale) Joost van Uffelen/Shutterstock.com; p. 9 (bottlenose dolphin) Action Sports Photography/Shutterstock.com; p. 9 (Amazon River dolphin) guentermanaus/ Shutterstock.com; p. 9 (Dalls porpoise) Daniel A. Leifheit/Moment/Getty Images; p. 9 (finless porpoise) The Asahi Shimbun/Contributor/Getty Images; p. 11 (dolphin) VladGavriloff/Shutterstock.com; p. 11 (porpoise) PETER PARKS/Staff/AFP/Getty Images; p. 13 (porpoise) China Photos/Stringer/ Getty Images News/Getty Images; p. 15 (dolphin) ChameleonsEye/Shutterstock.com; p. 15 (porpoise) Mark Caunt/Shutterstock.com; p. 17 Serge Vero/Shutterstock.com; p. 18 Potapov Alexander/ Shutterstock.com; p. 19 (porpoise) Visuals Unlimited, Inc./Solvin Zankl/Visuals Unlimited/Getty Images.

Printed in the United States of America

CPSIA compliance information: Batch #CS15GS: For further information contact Gareth Stevens, New York, New York at 1-800-542-2595.

CONTENTS

Boldface words appear in the glossary.

Making a Splash

A grayish animal leaps out of the ocean, splashing about in the water with its friends. It's too small to be a whale. Is it a dolphin or something else? Maybe it's a porpoise! If you've ever had trouble telling the two animals apart, read on to see how they're different.

5

Dolphins, porpoises, and whales are all marine **mammals** in the animal group Cetacea. The name "Cetacea" is from a Greek word that means "large sea creature." Dolphins and porpoises are much alike in size and shape, and many of them act the same way in the ocean.

DOLPHIN

PORPOISE

WHALE

7

Family Business

There are more than 30 different species, or kinds, of dolphin, which belong to part of an animal family called Delphinidae. Porpoises have six different species and are part of an animal family called Phocoenidae. Though they look similar, scientists say comparing them is like comparing cats to dogs!

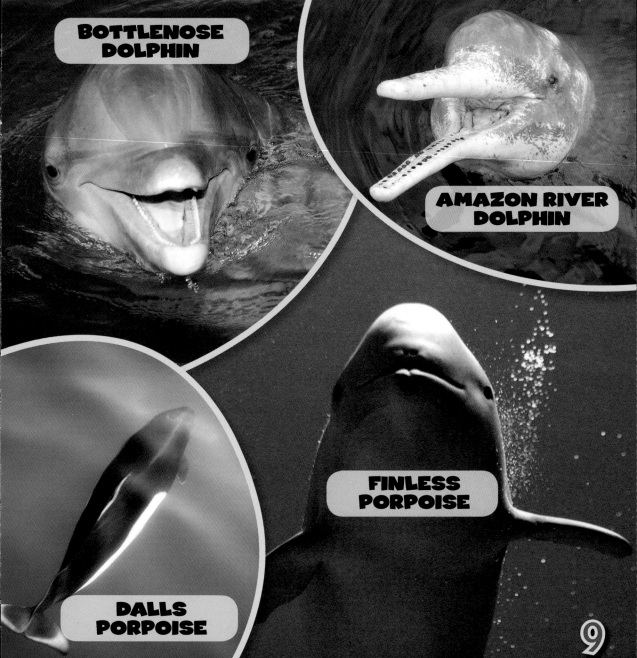

BOTTLENOSE
DOLPHIN

AMAZON RIVER
DOLPHIN

FINLESS
PORPOISE

DALLS
PORPOISE

9

All About Teeth

If you can catch a look inside their mouth, the best way to tell the difference between a porpoise and a dolphin is their teeth! Dolphins have cone-shaped teeth. Porpoises have flatter teeth that are **spade** shaped.

PORPOISE

DOLPHIN

How do you tell these mammals apart when they aren't showing their teeth? Their head shape is another clue. Dolphins have longer and larger beaks than porpoises. Dolphins also have thinner bodies, while porpoises look rounder.

DOLPHIN

PORPOISE

15

Dorsal Fins

Fins are important because they help dolphins and porpoises swim. The dorsal fin, which sits on their back, is slightly different for the two groups. Most porpoises have a triangle-shaped dorsal fin. The fin on dolphins is a more hooklike or curved shape.

PORPOISE
DORSAL FIN

DOLPHIN
DORSAL FIN

Chatterboxes

Dolphins love to "talk" to one another! They make clicks and noises with their **blowhole** we can hear with our ears. Scientists say that dolphins are more talkative than porpoises. However, porpoises make noises so high-pitched that humans can't hear them!

BLOWHOLE

Melon Heads

Dolphins and porpoises have something in their forehead called the melon. This helps them make **sonar** sound waves. Sonar waves leap off objects in the water and help dolphins and porpoises find their way around the ocean.

MELON

DOLPHIN

PORPOISE

HOW CAN YOU TELL?

ANIMAL	DOLPHIN	PORPOISE
FAMILY	Delphinidae	Phocoenidae
NUMBER OF SPECIES	more than 30	6
BEAK	long, big	short, small
BODY	thin	round
DORSAL FIN	hooked or curved	triangular
TEETH	cone shaped	spade shaped
NOISES	more "talkative"	less "talkative," or not at all

Watch Out!

Dolphins and porpoises are very smart animals with large brains. They'll **investigate** anything they're not used to in their **habitat**, so be careful when you're swimming in the ocean. You don't want to hurt these amazing animals!

GLOSSARY

blowhole: a body part on the top of the head of a dolphin or other sea mammal that allows it to breathe

habitat: the natural place where an animal or plant lives

investigate: to study closely

mammal: a warm-blooded animal that has a backbone, breathes air, and feeds milk to its young

sonar: sound waves used to find objects and move safely in a body of water

spade: a digging tool like a small shovel

FOR MORE INFORMATION

BOOKS

Clark, Willow. *Asian Dolphins and Other Marine Animals.* New York, NY: PowerKids Press, 2013.

Shaskan, Trisha Speed. *What's the Difference Between a Dolphin and a Porpoise?* Mankato, MN: Picture Window Books, 2011.

Silverman, Buffy. *Can You Tell a Dolphin from a Porpoise?* Minneapolis, MN: Lerner Publications, 2012.

WEBSITES

Dolphins and Porpoises

worldwildlife.org/species/dolphins-and-porpoises
Find out more about these animals and how you can help keep them safe.

What's the Difference Between Dolphins and Porpoises?

oceanservice.noaa.gov/facts/dolphin_porpoise.html
Find out more ways to tell these animals apart on this NOAA site.

INDEX